TO EARN THE SASH

PASSAGE TO DAWN: COMPANION

DERRICK SMYTHE

Dofean Press

Editor: Carolyn Haley
Cover Illustration: Alexandre Rito
Map Illustration: Daniel Hasenbos
Formatting: Derrick Smythe

ACKNOWLEDGMENTS

To my parents, who instilled in me the virtues of faith, respect, discipline, and integrity that formed the core of who I am today.

My mother fostered a love for the written word early in life, then later demonstrated that you're never too old to start something new, even if that new thing is marathon running. My father has been an inspiration to me and my siblings with his own brand of tirelessness, putting in countless overtime shifts in order to give us the best chance in life possible, never voicing a single complaint along the way.

To my older brother, who managed to captivate an easily distractible audience with his epic action-figure productions equipped with space crafts, backstory, and a long cast of characters with plot twists designed to cause his younger brothers to cry at the deaths of our favorite heroes.

To my eighth grade English teacher, Ms. Ryan, who likely had no idea how inspiring she was to my confidence as a writer, yet proved a pivotal hinge in my writing life in the years to follow.

To my alpha readers, Alex, Bryan, Dan, and Matt, all of whom provided invaluable feedback to improve this project.

To my editor, Carolyn, whose remarkable attention to detail provided more than just the critical polish prior to publication. To put it simply, a writer without an editor is like drywall without paint; and not all paint is created equal.

To Podium Audio for adapting this content to audio, and for allowing Alexandre to create another beautiful cover for this series.

To my wife, Kelly, whose frank critiques and enduring patience with me, not only as a writer but as a husband cannot be overstated, or over-thanked.

And finally, God, whose subtle nudges encouraged me to begin this journey in the first place, and who keeps me far from despair whenever things don't go according to my plan

AUTHOR'S NOTE

WHEN I INITIALLY COMPLETED THIS short-story, my intention was to release it as an eBook and audiobook only. It was written as an introduction to the Passage to Dawn series for those who might wish for a sample before diving into the full-volume books in the series. I also included Easter eggs that play into the main series as a whole to be enjoyed by those who have read some or all of the books thus far released.

When I finished writing in the fall of 2020, my wife begged me to release it in print.

I said, "No way. Who would want this in print? It's too short to even fit a proper title on the spine!"

We arrived at a compromise, I would offer printed copies for a limited time leading up to that Christmas season and put in one print-run of copies as a keepsake for friends, family, and superfans. One year later, after numerous requests for more, I have caved to the pressure. My wife has won. My fans have won. *To Earn the Sash* is now permanently available in print.

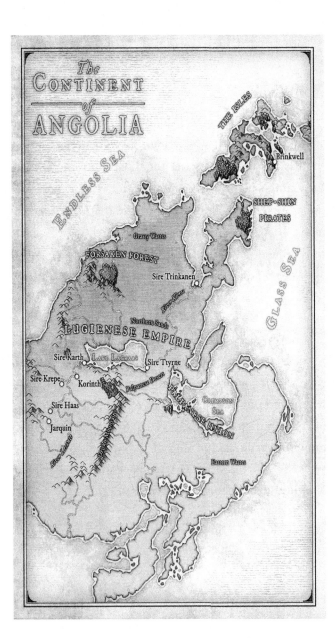

The
CONTINENT
of
ANGOLIA

ENDLESS SEA

THE ISLES

Brinkwell

SHEP-SHUN PIRATES

Grassy Wastes

FORSAKEN FOREST

Sire Trinkanen

River Kloss

GLASS SEA

Northern Sands

LUGIENESE EMPIRE

Sire Karth   LAKE LAGRAAS   Sire Ttyrne

Sire Krepe   Korinth

Sire Haas

Jarquin

River Lagraas

Palpanese Desert

PALPANESE UNION

OLYMPION SEA

Eastern Wastes

SEA OF SHARDS

THE ISLES

Tung

Green Sea

Mounthportu

Rynder

KINGDOM OF DOWE

BRONTORN

Varrامmen Desert

CITIES OF ORE

SWORDLORE TRIBES

Darkhook

Salmune

Quinson

East End

CITIES OF ANSHAN

Braxton

KAEL

Adonis

Pylis

Deva

HEDRAN CLANS

Dysodos

Scritler

Sari

Bemus

SCRITLAND

Novaya

SEA OF GLASS

Agyrus

BANGH-LIN

GLASS SEA

Luguinden Desert

Dadna

Ajman

Tal Afara

Desert of the Lost

Farah

LUGUINDEN CITY-STATES

Bajah

Ankar

Alluyah

Nineveh

Usak

SOTARIC SEA

SPRAIT OF SORROW

HAND OF THE GODS

KING OF THE SEA?

The
CONTINENT
of
DROGEN

ISLE OF BONES

CURSED ISLES

TO
EARN THE
SASH

CHAPTER 1

GROBENNAR

THE HIGH SEEKER'S VOICE RECITED the litany of rules yet again, but his words were drowned out by the thumping of Grobennar's pulse in his ears. The jitters of excitement strangled the young seeker's calm as he waited for the Annual Seekers Competition to begin.

Come on, pleaded Grobennar silently.

Hands at his side, he fluttered his fingers and shifted from one foot to the other in anticipation as he attempted to shake out the nervous tightness pulling at the back of each leg. Nothing helped. This redundancy insults us all. Just blow the horn already, thought Grobennar to himself. He attempted to release some of his tension through a series of measured breaths. Closing his eyes, he inhaled slowly, drawing in the cool morning air. *I am in control.* He repeated this process, relaxing as the tension melted away. *I am in control.* He opened his eyes as a gentle breeze blew across the city square, the robes of the other seekers billowing like banners set in tribute to the great God Klerós. The sun pierced the gaps between the surrounding city structures and the red fabric worn by Grobennar's competitors shimmered. It was beautiful. It was—

A nasally voice to Grobennar's left shattered his calm. The tall, slender priest named Rajuban snickered and said, "As if repeating these rules will be of any consequence."

I couldn't agree more, thought Grobennar, surprised to be in agreement with his long-standing adversary.

Rajuban continued, "This competition is already mine, after all."

And there it is.

"I'll have captured three of the hideous wretches before anyone else has sensed their first." Rajuban referred to tazamines, foul users of dark magic that had been staged throughout the city for the sake of the competition.

Grobennar was careful to keep his voice low as he furtively replied, "Your humility . . . such an endearing quality. It's a wonder you don't have more friends."

Rajuban turned his nose up even higher than was common for a one such as he. "A lecture on humility? How could I be anything but humble in the presence of the Grobennar? Rumor has it you gave birth to the

God-king yourself. Isn't that right?" He forced a few puffs from his lungs that loosely resembled laughter. Then added, "Don't you worry, I'll have plenty of friends once I wear the sash. Everyone else will merely wish they were my friends."

Oh, you could not be more wrong about that, thought Grobennar as he feigned curiosity about what the High Seeker had to say about the prohibition on employing magic against fellow priests during the competition.

Rajuban sniffed the air obnoxiously. "Ugh. What is that? It reeks. The scent of tazamines already? No— nope." He waved his hand in front of his face and wrinkled his nose. "Worse. It's the stench of your fear."

The stakes were indeed high. The best seekers-in-training from the Tathirean were assembled for a chance to earn the sash. This distinct honor would mean instantaneous graduation from the most prestigious academy in the Empire, as well as a one-year position as the first attendant to the High Seeker himself. Furthermore, it was well known that winners continued this trajectory within the Kleról, often earning positions within The Assembly.

Grobennar remained facing forward as he said, "You know, I hardly care to win for my own sake. But watching your smug expression melt away as tears of defeat streak your face . . . now that's a worthy cause."

Before Rajuban could respond, the horn blew and the competition was under way.

Blinding pain struck Grobennar's right knee and he stumbled to the ground, howling. Rajuban took off past him. "The rules don't prohibit attacks of the mundane, do they? I'm afraid I wasn't really listening." He continued to cackle as he disappeared into the crowd of competitors rushing foreward.

"You worm!" yelled Grobennar after him.

An ethereal voice resounded within Grobennar's mind. "Shall I heal you?"

"Yes," whined Grobennar.

"Very well," said Jaween, the spirit within the red multifaceted gemstone worn around Grobennar's neck.

The sixteen-year-old priest sighed in relief as the pain in his knee dissipated.

"You know, we could always just kill him. Accidents happen all the time, especially during the chaos of organized competition. No one would have to—"

"We're not killing anyone. I'm late to my rendezvous." Grobennar scrambled to his feet and sprinted toward the place where he and his team of compatriots would join forces to locate the tazamines.

He was panting when he arrived at the alley just off the main bazaar of Sire Karth's mercantile district.

Grobennar was the youngest priest in the academy by several years, but he was a known prodigy and his plan to win was simple: convince others to help. In exchange, he had promised reciprocation once in a position of power. With Grobennar having already proven himself more skilled than the rest, save perhaps Rajuban, it was wise for those with political ambitions to accept his offer of alliance.

Nine out of the twenty-four priests in their cohort were waiting for him in the alley.

"What happened? Get lost?" asked Penden, a friend since their first post in the priesthood together. "I figured your little legs would only be a few paces behind my own."

Grobennar was beginning to catch his breath. "Never mind that. We've got a competition to win."

He wasted no time in extending his hands. The others did the same, forming a human chain in the shape of an oval within the narrow alleyway.

Grobennar felt the flows of energy grow even as he extended his mind to take hold of them. It was like standing outside as the sun peeked out from behind the clouds. The power grew rapidly and he drank in as much as he could safely handle. Then he set it to work, a net of sensitivity far stronger and detailed than what any one of them could have cast alone. Grobennar soon held in his mind's eye a detailed mental map of every expulsion of dark magic within the city. A limited number of tazamines were kept alive for the sole purpose of training seekers. Twenty-three had been positioned around the city today, coerced into using their magic as part of the competition. Grobennar could sense their presence as distinctly as if each was a blazing fire in the darkness of night.

Grobennar shared their locations with the members of his assemblage, then split the four weakest priests into two teams of two, while he and the rest went individually to recover their prey.

CHAPTER 2

RAJUBAN

RAJUBAN DASHED PAST AN ADVERSARIAL priestess as he neared the closest tazamine. "Pardon," he sneered at the girl.

She let out a curse then cut around a cart and through a crowd and was suddenly out in front of Rajuban once again.

Blast that little speed demon.

The tazamine they sought was now in clear sight; a slave-breed out in the open at the center of the small market square, guarded by an ordained seeker.

Rajuban gritted his teeth as he pulled out the rope that would be used to bind the tazamine. Only, he gripped the magic-infused cuff designed to snap shut around the neck of a tazamine. It would have been illegal to use the magical clasp against another student, but the other end was merely a fine piece of rope. He worked skilled hands to create a slipknot from the rope end, and just before the priestess reached out to claim her prize, Rajuban threw.

The makeshift lasso flew over the priestess's head and encircled her neck . . . Rajuban yanked with stunning force. Her feet swung up into the air and she crashed to the ground, gagging and coughing. Rajuban quickly reached her and loosened the knot to remove it so he could claim his second tazamine of the day. "You chose the wrong side," he growled. Then he kicked her in the stomach just for good measure.

"You—you—you're a . . ." She broke into a fit of coughing, grasping at her partially collapsed trachea.

The ordained seeker guarding the tazamine said nothing about the action, but his disapproving scowl was unmistakable. Rajuban had not violated the rules of the competition, but many would view his tactics as dishonorable. Yet when he won, he would care nothing for this man's opinion. Rajuban would outrank the man in a matter of hours. Fool.

Rajuban quickly reached the city square to deliver the tazamine. This one, like most, possessed the reddish-brown skin and blond hair of a slave-breed. Nevertheless, whatever rebellious tendencies he might have once possessed had long since been eradicated by the Kleról. Rajuban undid the clasp at its wrist, and it slinked over to one of the two caged wagons. Rajuban grinned as the chime of a bell announced his success. He could feel the tingle of magic employed by the first-year trainees whose sole responsibility was to create the illuminated orbs that mark the number of captured tazamines above each competitor's banner. He glanced over at the only banner that mattered and saw two orange lights hovering above it.

Right on track. He started toward the next-closest tazamine he had sensed within the city.

Just then he heard the chime of another bell and turned to see Grobennar release his own tazamine, his banner lighting up with another orb.

Rajuban scowled. This is going to be closer than I thought. Grobennar's collaborative effort was indeed making the contest difficult. But Grobennar wasn't the only one who had made alliances; he was just the only one who hadn't tried to hide it, a mistake the 'blessed' boy would very soon regret.

A single green burst of light shot high into the sky a few streets to the east, a signal meant to notify Rajuban that an ally had captured a tazamine on his behalf.

Then he felt a flash of pagan magic nearby. Rajuban smiled to himself.

The seeker guarding the tazamine had forced it to call upon its dark power again in order to alert nearby competitors. These tazamines were kept alive and even trained for just such a purpose and knew better than to disobey.

Rajuban started toward this new quarry just as two classmates emerged from a side street up ahead, both allies of Grobennar. Rajuban redoubled his effort, but quickly realized that they were too swift for him to overtake.

His mind absorbed the surroundings in a split second, evaluating each option available. "Time to bend the rules yet again," he said to himself, and laughed.

Careful to avoid violating the statutes of the competition by employing magic against either boy directly, Rajuban shot a sliver of magical energy to zip just past them. They shouted in surprise as a canvas awning fell upon them; the main support had 'somehow' collapsed.

"Oops." Rajuban muttered as he sprinted past screams of "Cheater!" and "Thief!"

Rajuban claimed his tazamine, then sent a shock of pinching energy into his newly acquired companion, convincing the otherwise lethargic slave-breed to run so Rajuban could make haste in collecting the other. A short while later, Rajuban had two orbs of light added to his board. He was now leading by one, and his last trap had yet to be sprung.

This is really happening. He shook his head. Don't celebrate until you wear the sash. Then he dashed off in the other direction; he still needed to secure at least one more on his own.

He couldn't help but smile as he saw Grobennar sprint past empty-handed. "Don't worry, I'm sure you'll find another," yelled Rajuban after the departing form.

CHAPTER 3

GROBENNAR

GROBENNAR SCOWLED AT RAJUBAN'S TAUNTS but knew he would be better served by keeping to the task at hand and not verbal distractions intended only to fluster.

"Just a small mental intrusion?" begged Jaween in Grobennar's head.

"Not unless you want me to lose my robes."

"Rules, rules. Who would believe Rajaja, anyway?"

"It would only take one ordained priest to call for an investigation."

"I could persssssuade him to end his own life. Problem solved. Dead humans speak very little."

"How about we win this competition and let the sash do the talking?" replied Grobennar. Anything besides this was energy wasted. That included meaningless arguments with Jaween.

"Now hush!"

Jaween slunk back into the recesses of Grobennar's mind, but he could feel the displeasure through the link.

Grobennar slid around a corner and nearly bumped into another red-robed shape, a competing priest who turned back and gave a sinister smile. Rajuban. How had he gotten in front of him? Then he saw that Rajuban was not only smiling because he was ahead. He held out a leather pouch, then upturned it, dropping a handful of—

Grobennar's feet slid out from beneath him, and he felt sharp bites of pain all over his toppled form. He rolled to his stomach and felt more of the sharp objects cut into his hands. Coming to his feet, he examined his hands and pulled out a shard of glass, blood running even faster from the now-exposed wound. Rajuban! The priest had emptied a pouch of marbles mixed with broken glass! The lengths he took to win!

"A little help?"

"As you wish. And . . . my other offer still sta—"

Grobennar released a bellow and Jaween discontinued his question in lieu of healing Grobennar's cuts.

I will not lose to him. I will not. And a small part of him did actually consider Jaween's offer, if only for a moment.

He ran off toward the next-closest tazamine. There weren't many remaining and it was going to be close, but he had recently felt the magical bursts of his allies, notifying him that he had two more tazamines to gather. If he could secure this last one on his own, he could still win.

With great joy Grobennar delivered this last tazamine and saw that he was now tied with Rajuban. He did a quick count and confirmed that with just two more of the competition's staged tazamines remaining, his victory was all but assured.

He jogged confidently to the place where his allies waited with the last two. Paranja stood off to the side, seated casually along the edge of a fountain marking the entrance to Old Town, a well-maintained section of Sire Karth occupied by the older, wealthier families. She was looking pleased with herself as she lifted the rope that tethered the slight female tazamine beside her. Paranja was a considerably talented seeker who was already an ordained priestess of healing, but she felt called to also earn the sash of the seeker. A pair of less-talented yet resourceful seekers, Paetar and Keldri, stood side by side between two buildings to the left of the fountain, looking awkward as always, but behind them crouched the form of the last tazamine.

Grobennar raised a fist in triumph. "We've done it!"

No longer in a hurry, he strolled over to Paranja, who handed him the confused tazamine's rope.

"Thank you, Paranja."

She smiled and nodded. "My pleasure."

Then Grobennar continued over toward Paetar and Keldri.

Against the nearest building to Grobennar's left, leaned an uninterested ordained seeker named Theron. He had been a great help to Grobennar early in his training at the Tathirean. Grobennar expected a word of praise for his victory, but Razir Theron didn't so much as meet his eyes. *That's odd. Perhaps he disapproves of the use of alliances.*

That's when Grobennar noticed that Paetar had moved his hands behind his back, and the priestess, Keldri, moved to bar the way.

Grobennar rolled his eyes. "This is no time for games. Step aside."

Keldri held firm, then blocked his attempt to step around her.

"Oh, this is no game, friend." Rajuban's nasally voice was like a potent smell catching him unawares. Grobennar spun to see the thin, older youth gliding forward, smug as ever.

What is going on here? he wondered, though he had a sinking suspicion that he knew.

Rajuban chuckled. "You didn't think you could make allies of half of the class and not have any defectors, did you?"

Grobennar turned to glare at Paetar, whom he had believed to be a friend. "How could you?"

Paetar opened his mouth to speak but said nothing, and Rajuban spoke again as he came to stand beside the traitor. "Don't blame the lad. This isn't his fault, not really. Everyone has their price."

Looking Paetar in the eyes, Grobennar said, "I will not forget this, ever."

Paetar dropped his gaze, and again it was Rajuban who responded. "No, I suspect you won't. And someday you'll thank me for teaching you this lesson."

Rajuban snatched up the rope, and Grobennar realized there was still a chance to win. In the event of a tie, victory was determined by the best time. He could still win this if he hurried!

As if reading his thoughts, Paetar and Keldri stepped forward to grab his robes. He spun away, but was still holding the rope to his tazamine and the pair quickly caught him once again.

Grobennar looked up and met Theron's gaze. "Please! Help!"

Theron shrugged his shoulders and looked away unsympathetically. Of course they could. Rajuban had simply out maneuvered him. There was nothing in the rules to prohibit this. Grobennar's own allies might have done the same thing should the roles have been reversed.

Rajuban took off at a jog with his cargo. "See you at the ceremony, ol' pal. Oh, and I'll put in a good word for you as I rise through the Kleról ranks, several steps ahead."

Paranja attempted to help free Grobennar, but she was nearly as small as he. It was no use.

Jaween shouted into his mind, "Let me at them. Just a few moments!" But it was too late, and the thought that he would be excommunicated should Jaween's presence be discovered was the only reason Grobennar held the spirit in check. He couldn't let his emotions convince him to betray the rest of his future, no matter how dim it currently appeared.

Paetar and Keldri released their hold and Grobennar fell to the ground, still clinging to the rope tethering his tazamine. Paranja helped him up and Grobennar brushed the dirt from his red robes. His old friend Paetar had the nerve to offer an apology, but Grobennar didn't acknowledge it. The traitor didn't deserve even that much of Grobennar's attention.

He trudged back toward the grounds where he would turn over the tazamine, for no other reason now than to be rid of the abomination. As he walked, purposeless step after purposeless step toward the humiliation of having lost in spite of the alliances he had garnered in support of his victory, he heard an almost buzzing sound in his head, and finally realized that it was Jaween.

"What is it?"

"Mmmm? Oh, nothing. I was just, well, I think I'm feeling sad for you . . ."

This is new, thought Grobennar. "You don't feel things."

"Mmmm true. But I still wish there was something else I could have done, like dropping a very large rock on Rajaja's head. It should be you who rises to the top, not him."

"Yes, well, there was really nothing you could have done short of revealing yourself. Not unless you could conjure up some more tazamines for me to turn over, which considering they have a set amount wouldn't mat—" He recalled an image of the rules, written as they were. He did a mental scan from memory, searching for any clarifying language, but the phraseology was quite vague; no doubt an attempt to simplify the process. "I think there might be a way . . ."

"Oh? Do tell? Does it include persssuasion?"

"No."

"Blast!"

"But I'll need your help."

"Oh goody."

Grobennar headed back toward the fountain where he had just retrieved his tazamine and twirled his finger to the sky in thanks to Klerós that Razir Theron had taken the same route.

"Razir Theron, I'm returning this tazamine to your care."

Theron furrowed his brows. "What?"

"Exactly what I said, I'm returning this tazamine to your care."

Theron shook his head and sighed. "Tadi Grobennar, it's been a long day. He beat you, now be a sport and finish with dignity."

Grobennar grinned. "That is precisely my intention. Just . . ." He looked to the sky and guessed he had another hour before the final bell rang to announce the official end to the competition. "I just need you to hold on to this thing for a little while longer. Can you do that?"

Razir Theron gave him a look of annoyance but held out his hand to take the rope. "Very well, but know this. I will be turning it over to the headmaster before that final bell tolls, so you'd best hurry doing . . . whatever it is you intend to do."

Grobennar raced toward the western edges of Sire Karth, where he knew two-fifths of all tazamines in the last five years had been discovered. As he drew near, he found a quiet, empty alley and sank down to the ground, his back against the wall.

He reached up and clutched the pendant housing the spirit. "Okay, time to pay up for all the time you've spent occupying space around my neck."

"I would argue that our relationship is what the potion mixers call symbiotic. But I do enjoy being helpful. And I looove catching tazamines."

Grobennar summoned Klerós's power, then extended his mind outward in search of any hints of sorcery lingering in the air. In spite of the Kleról's tight control and skilled seekers, not every tazamine was discovered. Many could survive for years, some because they had few episodes of manifestation, others because they learned to hide or control their evil taint. Either way, Grobennar was praying he might find such a one in time to win this competition.

He felt his sensitivity to magic grow as Jaween pushed some of his own power through their connection, and he continued to survey the surrounding area for any residual evidence of magic having been used. Seeking was often compared to the sense of smell, and while it was a fair analogy, Grobennar felt it more accurate to compare seeking to sight. That was perhaps because his heightened sensitivity allowed him to detect a relative location better than any seeker he knew. And that was before he realized he could use Jaween to enhance his skills.

"There." He held the position in his mind's eye then traced a mental line back to his current location.

"Oh joyous day, we're going to win!"

"That's only if we can find the tazamine responsible for this magical residue. This is so faint, it's at least two days old. And we still have to get the thing back to the square before the bell chimes."

"I'm not the one with a body here, but shouldn't you be running?"

Grobennar had already started.

Minutes later he skidded to a halt in front of a tanner's shop. With no time to worry over catching his breath, he pushed through the door. Several sets of eyes turned to regard him, round in surprise both at the abrupt entry and the seeker robes, for—sash or no sash—he would not be one to trifle with.

The shop's tanner, a Lugienese man dressed in a brown commoner's tunic, recovered his composure and said, "Greetings, Razir. Is there . . . something I can help you with?"

Grobennar continued to scan the room for the remnants of magic used, but they were so faint he could discern no more than this general area as the place of use. Time to smoke out the truth. "I was notified that dark magic has been employed here. I came to investigate."

The two prospective buyers set down the boots they had been handling and backed away from the tanner.

The tanner's eyes went wide, and he seemed so sincerely astonished that Grobennar almost believed it was genuine, which is why he concluded that it was not. *It has to be him. He was middle aged so he had been hiding it for decades.*

"You two. Leave now. You, tanner. What is your name?"

The man gave an awkward, squeaky laugh. "I—my name is Lorendar, my Razir." Then he turned to the departing couple and said, "This is but a misunderstanding. Please, Mr. and Mrs. Jonas, do return tomorrow. This will all be sorted out by then."

They hastily departed.

Grobennar walked forward, focusing all of his attention on the man to see if he could get a sense of wrongness from him; but without using magic now, Grobennar could not be certain, and he didn't have time to conduct the kind of investigation the Kleról might do in such a case.

"I'm not certain that it is him."

"Nor am I, but we're going to have to take our chances. I'm nearly out of time."

Lorendar looked at him as if he was insane. Grobennar grimaced. *I am talking out loud to a spirit trapped within a pendant worn at my neck!* He supposed the tanner's reaction was appropriate.

"You will come with me—now. Resist, and I will not hesitate to inflict great harm." He drew in Klerós's power and pressed it against the man's skin to create a slight burning sensation as a warning. Unlike the tazamines they used for training, that had been beaten to the point of extreme docility, Grobennar knew that wild tazamines could be completely unpredictable, and he did not have the time for such games.

"Jaween, be ready to persuade should he need it."

"Oooh yesss. Oh please do resist, dear Lorendar. Please do!"

The man's eyes darted from side to side before he said loudly, "Okay. I will do as you say, my Razir. Everything will be all right. This is just a misunderstanding. Not to worry."

"Good," responded Grobennar. But something was off. *This is too easy.*

Lorendar started walking around the counter where he had been standing at the back of the small shop. As he did so, one of his arms remained at his side, hand below the counter. Something about that was wrong. A weapon, perhaps?

Grobennar took a few more steps toward him and yelled, "Hands where I can see them!"

Lorendar did as asked but started to move away from the counter.

"There is another here," warned Jaween.

That's when Grobennar saw the sprouts of hair, the top of someone's head previously hidden by the waist-high counter.

"Stop!" yelled Grobennar.

The man froze in place, but his pleading eyes followed Grobennar as he approached the counter.

"Who's this?"

The head moved and two beady eyes peered up at him, afraid. Then the child skittered to hide behind the man.

Grobennar met the tanner's gaze and saw his expression go from fearful to pleading. "Please," he whimpered. "Leave the girl. Take me."

"What is her name?"

"Please," repeated the hoarse voice.

"What is her name!" Grobennar yelled.

"N—N—Nimrey," Lorendar squeaked.

Grobennar spoke in as gentle a voice as he could under the circumstances. "Nimrey. Everything is going to be all right. But I need you to be brave and come out from behind your da."

She poked her head out and slowly stepped forward. The tanner was shaking. "Please . . ." he whispered once again.

The girl shuffled forward, and Grobennar drew on Jaween's power to magnify his search for any remnant that might connect this girl to the taint of dark magic that had drawn him to this place.

Then he felt the tingling sensation of magic being drawn. That left no doubt.

Grobennar pulled the rope out with his left hand and prepared his right hand to capture the girl.

"It's not her," said Jaween.

Jaween was right—the magic was coming from her father. Lorendar lifted his hands. "Take me." Before he could complete whatever it was he attempted, Grobennar shot a blast of air at his chest. Not hard enough to kill, but enough to break his grip on what little power he could wield. The man was thrown back into the wall and, to Grobennar's relief, his magic evaporated.

Lorendar sank to his knees and held out hands. "Please, take me."

Grobennar snapped the magic cuffs around his wrists behind his back.

Then Grobennar pulled out another clasping rope. Tazamine magic, while seemingly random, was often found to be hereditary, and Grobennar had seen enough of a faint coating on the girl to deduce that he had been drawn there by the leftovers of magic she had employed, not the father who, unlike many slave-breed tazamines, appeared to be able to control his.

"I beg you," he pleaded.

Grobennar stared at Nimrey and said, "She too has the Dark Lord's taint."

Grobennar saw a small puff of dust stir as the man's tear struck the hard-packed floor.

CHAPTER 4

RAJUBAN

SIRE KARTH BAKED BENEATH THE gaze of an angry afternoon sun. The air grew thick and stagnant as if the Dark Lord himself had opened his maw from above, rank breath settling in the streets like a fog. The High Seeker held the golden sash out for Rajuban, his forehead glistening with sweat as he addressed the assembly of prospective seekers. He droned on from behind the pulpit, a monotone stream of words that could take on meaning only if you were able to maintain focus long enough to absorb them in their entirety. "It is a great honor and responsibility to don the sash of an ordained seeker, and a greater reward still to work directly beneath the Fatu Razir."

Yes, yes, get on with it already.

Rajuban stepped toward the lectern to claim his prize, then glanced back hoping to see Grobennar among the disappointed faces in attendance. Rajuban had urged the razir in charge of the competition to hold off on beginning the ceremony until the final bell had chimed, as he wished to ensure that Grobennar witnessed him placing the sash around his neck. However, Fatu Razir Herododar, the High Seeker in whose employ Rajuban would begin on the morrow, was in a hurry to return to the Kleról and saw no reason for delay.

The golden satin sash of the seeker was on its way into Rajuban's hands but never made it. A shout rang out from behind the assembled seekers. It was Grobennar's voice: "The bell has not chimed!"

The entire audience turned to regard the young seeker-in-training who strode forward leading the remaining tazamine and . . . a large man dressed in a tunic and the jerkin of some sort of tradesman? Yet both wore the seeker clasp around their wrists.

"What are you about, Tadi Razir Grobennar?" queried an annoyed Razir Jerikor, the priest directly in charge of the academy and this ritual. "The competition is over."

Grobennar shook his head in defiance. "The criterion for victory is clear; the priest who returns with the most tazamines from within the city, before the chiming of the final bell, is the winner. The bell has not yet chimed—or did I miss that?"

Razir Jerikor puffed out his chest as he approached Grobennar, aggravated at having the ceremony interrupted in front of the Fatu Razir, his direct superior. "There were precisely twenty-one tazamines staged within the city. They are the qualifying targets. This last captive puts you even with Tadi Razir Rajuban at six, and because he returned first, section II, clause IV dictates that he is the victor. Don't jeopardize your future within the Kleról by making a spectacle of your defeat. Take the loss with grace."

Rajuban's fists had tightened into the smallest versions of themselves possible, but he relaxed them at Razir Jerikor's words. Thank you very much, Jerikor.

To everyone's surprise, Grobennar foolishly stepped up to the platform with his captives and looked not at Razir Jerikor but at the Fatu Razir. "The intent of what is written may have been meant to apply only to qualified, training tazamines placed neatly throughout the city; however, the language itself does not specifically state this. I will recite the most pertinent sections if it please you, but I would prefer to assume that you know the words and can simply confirm that I speak the truth on this matter." Grobennar paused, waiting to be disputed, but when nothing was said, he nodded and continued. "I petition that with the capture of an additional tazamine from within the city before the chiming of the bell, I now have seven qualifying tazamines, and have therefore satisfied the requirements for victory. It is I who should be granted the sash of the razir."

He bowed his head in deference to Fatu Razir Herododar, then knelt, offering him the ropes holding his captives.

Razir Jerikor pointed a finger, fuming at having been ignored. "How dare—"

"Silence!" boomed the Fatu Razir. "Tadi Razir Grobennar has addressed me, not you."

Everything went absolutely still and the stifling weight of these words hung in the humid air threatening to crush Rajuban, who would have been certain that his heart had stopped working if it weren't for the rhythmic pounding in his temples.

He can't actually be considering the validity of such nonsense!

But the Fatu Razir had brought his hand to his chin and began to pace up and down the platform behind the lectern. He did so for an uncomfortable period of time before finally stopping before the man Grobennar had brought forth as a tazamine. The Fatu Razir inspected the tanner, who shrank under the weight of scrutiny. Speaking softly enough that only those closest could hear, Fatu Razir muttered, "Certainly does have the taint, though it's extremely faint. I can't even begin to guess how you managed to find him, and under the pressure of competition, yet. Remarkable . . . yes, I have made my decision."

No. This cannot be happening, thought Rajuban.

Fatu Razir spun on his heel, robes whirling, and with a finger raised to the sky, proclaimed, "Razir

Jerikor. You will tighten up the language in the rules of the competition to specify that only tazamines selected by the Kleról will count toward the final tally."

Rajuban felt relief wash over him.

But the Fatu Razir continued addressing the onlookers, "However, with the rules written as they are today, I cannot deny the ingenuity of a priest who works to maximize his effect through the letter of such law, a true scholar, a visionary, just the sort of man we need during times like these."

No. No. No—no—nooo! The fruit of Rajuban's labor had been inches from his hands, and was still just a short reach away, and yet Grobennar had stolen it from him. The Fatu Razir continued speaking, but Rajuban heard nothing. His mind bled with the ache of dreams deferred and the anger born out of hate incarnate.

CHAPTER 5

GROBENNAR

GROBENNAR FELT AS IF HE were being lifted by invisible wings, floating toward the Fatu Razir, who now offered the sash to him. Grobennar took it in his hands and gingerly positioned it around his neck, to hang down the front of his filthy red robes. Several in the group cheered as he turned to face them, while others who had been in league with Rajuban or had gone at it alone merely clapped absently, unhappy with the result but obliged to accept it.

Grobennar had prepared for his reward; he worked hard to hone his skills so that he might be able to achieve the sash. But to stand where he was, the youngest ever to earn the robes, and again to have won the seeker competition, he felt there was nothing he could not accomplish.

The Fatu Razir raised a hand to calm the noise, then spoke again. "We live in a time of unprecedented prominence, an era that will bring about great change throughout the land. For the prophesied God-king walks among us. He who will bring the world to its knees before Klerós himself; he who has been sent to eradicate the darkness of this world dwells among us now. But"—he brought his voice back to a calm, collected level, and his fingers clasped together over his slight stomach—"our Magog is only a child. Not yet strong in his power. He must be groomed. He must be shown the way. He has, of course, many tutors, but the council has discussed and agreed that he needs more. A guide who would form a lasting relationship and foster growth unlike that which is ordinarily known between master and student. What better selection than the very one who was responsible for the miraculous fulfillment of this very prophecy years ago? Who better to fulfill this role than our newest ordained seeker, Razir Grobennar?"

Grobennar felt his face flush with excitement. "You honor me with such a responsibility. I will take on this role with great reverence and joy."

"You're not going to mess this up, are you?" teased Jaween.

Grobennar hated to admit it, but Jaween had a point. This was an immense responsibility. This was the sort of thing that would either propel Grobennar to the top or erase everything he had accomplished thus far and more. And yet, wasn't that the case for any feat of greatness? How much had he risked when he took the life of a senior priest in order to bring Magog's birth to fruition? Had he failed in the aftermath, he would have been burned at the stake, and that's if the Kleról had been feeling merciful.

This is my destiny, he said to himself. *I must not give in to self-doubt, or Jaween-inspired doubt.*

The Fatu Razir clapped his hands happily and held both up to quiet the murmurs throughout the assembled prospective seekers. "The unusual outcome of today's competition is merely another sign of Klerós working in our midst. For I am able to satisfy the needs of the Kleról to the fullest extent during a time when I had yet to decide the course best suited for this situation." He turned back to address Rajuban. "Razir . . . I'm sorry, what was your name again?"

Rajuban seemed not to hear, but Razir Jerikor offered his name and the Fatu Razir continued, "Tadi Razir Rajuban."

This time Rajuban did look up, confusion written on his face. Grobennar was equally flummoxed. "Tadi Razir Rajuban, you were the winner of today's competition, or you would have been, had your opponent been anyone but the extraordinary young man beside you. Razir Grobennar's new role will limit his ability to satisfy the role of personal attendant to me, and it is within my power today to offer you this position as well as the sash you would have otherwise earned."

"He's going to be right on your heels as you rise to power. Should have just killed him."

Grobennar swore under his breath. He hated to admit it, but the crazy spirit was probably right, not that Grobennar could have actually done such a thing. It was one thing to kill in the name of Klerós, but to kill for his own ambition? That was beyond him

CHAPTER 6

RAJUBAN

RAJUBAN HAD SOME CHOICE WORDS and perhaps a little more than just words to share with the 'blessed' Grobennar, who had once again stolen his glory. But he held back his approach as Grobennar took an unusual path back to their quarters within the Tathirean.

What is he up to now? wondered Rajuban, who had long suspected that something was slightly, or perhaps very, off about the child 'prodigy.' Keeping a safe distance between himself and the slight priest wearing the new sash, Rajuban continued toward the western reaches of the Sire Karth, a place occupied by the common working folk, shopkeepers, and tradesmen. Grobennar entered one such shop and disappeared from view.

Rajuban stalked along and peeked in the front window.

He spotted Grobennar standing with his back to the window, and a woman off to the side, a child huddling behind her. The woman pointed an accusatory finger at Grobennar, who shook his head.

Rajuban ducked below the window and shuffled along toward the door. He needed to hear what was being said. When he got to the door, he took the handle and turned it ever so slightly, then pushed it slowly, just a crack.

"You've already taken my husband, now you wish to take my daughter? She's not what you say!"

"I'm afraid she is. In fact, she is what drew me here in the first place," said Grobennar.

"No. You're mistaken—not her. Lorendar would have told me," the woman cried.

"Perhaps he wished to shield you from the danger of knowing, hoping he could teach her to control it, to hide it as he had learned to do himself. Whatever the case, this child is a tazamine, and I have come here to spare her a life as a tazamine training subject. I offer mercy."

Grobennar the merciful? How very interesting. Not so devout now, is he?

"Hand her over and let's be done with this. I do not relish the task, but it is what I promised her father. I will use the power granted to me by Klerós to restrain you if I must."

The woman was sobbing. "Please," she whimpered, and Rajuban could hear the child's cries, too.

Rajuban backed away from the door as Grobennar did the deed. He would wait until they were well away from this place before he let his little friend know that he had been caught, and see how he might leverage this to his advantage.

Grobennar strode out of the tanner's shop, his gait one of authority and confidence, but the facade shrank away only a few steps from the threshold of the door. The boy's shoulders now slumped as if carrying a heavy pack.

Only a short walk later, Grobennar ducked into an alley. Rajuban had been on the streets long enough to know this trick. Grobennar must have somehow noticed that he was being followed and hoped to catch his pursuer unawares. Rajuban was no fool. He knew this part of the city well and darted down a parallel street. He'd sneak up from the other side behind the lad, and then they could have their little chat.

Rajuban peered cautiously into the alley, but what he saw was not what he expected.

Grobennar was sitting with his back to the alley wall, head between his legs, and he was . . . crying? Yes, he was crying—sobbing, actually.

So pathetic, thought Rajuban. And yet, you lost to this whimpering child. Shut up! Rajuban scolded himself.

The sound of Grobennar's voice interrupted the divisive inner monologue. "She was just a girl! Not a slave. A true-blood!"

Grobennar's voice echoed throughout the alley, making it easy for Rajuban to hear.

"I know it had to be done, but—yeah, well, I'm a human. Yes, I know what the Kleról says. Since when did you care? You desire only chaos and death."

Is he talking to himself? The boy is mad.

Grobennar continued, "No, that would have been worse. Don't you see? I did not want the girl to suffer!"

Then he saw the boy reach up to take hold of the pendant he always wore about his neck. He held it up as he spoke, as if speaking to it. But that couldn't be.

"I don't need you anymore. I can do this without you. Shut up and let me be!"

Either Grobennar is insane, or he is actually speaking to someone . . . or . . . something. But who? What?

"I don't care about Rajuban right now."

Rajuban froze. Had he been seen? But Grobennar was still facing forward, staring at the red rubied pendant clutched in his hand.

"Wait, here? Where?"

Grobennar stiffened, then slowly turned to face him. Rajuban ducked back behind the building. He was pretty sure he had not been seen. He was also pretty sure he had witnessed yet another thing he was not supposed to see.

He ran.

There were several possible explanations for what he had just witnessed, some far less ruinous to Grobennar than others. Rajuban had much more to consider. Revealing his cards now might be premature. Rajuban was a strategist, always playing the long game. And what he had just learned about Grobennar could be something with interesting implications.

CHAPTER 7

GROBENNAR

RAJUBAN WORE A DARK BROWN traveling cloak, hood drawn. He sat patiently waiting for the boys and girls to exit the Kleról's school for children, a place where all children learned the virtues of Klerós while also being screened for aptitude as potential wielders of the priesthood.

Had Grobennar not been admitted to the Kleról so much sooner than was appropriate for one so young, he would have been here even now. The boy had grown up in one of the poorest quarters of Sire Karth, outside the original city walls, built before the spike in drogal trade and the subsequent population surge.

The academy would release children before midday so they could return to helping their families with whatever they did to provide food and shelter for themselves in this place. Rajuban had approached the Kazi priest on his way into the small building earlier. Kazi Ferodan, having bottomed out in his career as a teacher in one of the lowliest of places possible for an ordained member of the Kleról, was amenable to Rajuban's requests; especially with the promise of a generous transfer of duties, should the outcome of his questioning prove useful.

As midday approached and the children were released, Kazi Ferodan pulled two of the older boys aside and returned them to their seats as Rajuban entered.

Rajuban nodded toward the door of the simple place. "These questions are of a sensitive nature."

Kazi Ferodan closed the door, then made introductions. The boys were named Lorenor and Hector.

Rajuban removed his traveling cloak to reveal his station as an ordained seeker, and first attendant to the Fatu Razir. The boys straightened and squirmed.

"Gentlemen, I would first like to assure you that you are in no trouble. However, it is my understanding that you may have information that could prove extremely valuable to the Kleról, and the reward for your assistance in such a matter will be quite handsome." He pulled out a thick golden coin, and began performing a dexterous dance along his fingers with a piece of currency larger than either had likely seen in their lives. Their eyes went wide and they leaned forward eagerly.

"I am curious to learn what you know about the red amulet worn by an old acquaintance of yours, the one known as Grobennar." The boys looked at each other, confused, though Rajuban was uncertain by which part of the question.

He continued, "We fear he may be in some danger and would like to help him, but we have to know more about how he came to own such a curious trinket."

The boys shrugged, but Rajuban noticed the smaller boy to the right, squirming slightly in his seat. This one was called Hector, and he knew something.

"I should also like to remind you that you are speaking with the first attendant to the Fatu Razir, and should it be found out that you are hiding something, anything at all, the penalty will be severe." He said this with eyes boring down upon Hector, who gulped as his face lost color.

Then, to Rajuban's delight, the boy cleared his throat and said in a shaky voice, "I—I know where he got it."

Rajuban did his best to provide a warm, comforting smile. "I'm so happy to hear this. Please go on."

The boy nodded shakily and gulped again. "A while back, me, Grobennar, and Jed, we was playing out there by Lesante's Scar—I mean—I'm sorry—I mean the prophetess no disrespect. I just don't know the proper name, and that's what us folks here call it, you know. It's a ravine west of the river. There's a small creek there where lots of the children play, you know, when our chores is done. But, well, we was there and lookin' fer flat rocks, you know, makin' a dam in the stream as we was."

"Now, I should also tell you that we was a little further west than we normally play. We was in the gorge itself, where we been warned not to be for the bad spirits that live there."

Rajuban interrupted, "Bad spirits?"

The boy blushed and tipped his head down. "That's what my ma told me. Told me never to go in the gorge 'cause there be bad spirits in there. But Jed said this was nonsense, that she just didn't want us wandering too far. But my ma's not the only one who said that place was bad. Lots say so."

Rajuban rolled his eyes. "Continue."

"Well, we told Jed we didn't want to go so far west, but he was older, and callin' us sissies. I know that's no excuse, but we followed. And after we was there a while, he called us over to see this rock he lifted up. It was perfect and flat, but that's not why he done called us over. There was a hole underneath, you see. Big enough for a man to climb down into.

"I was scared outta my wits and stayed up above. Couldn't've paid me enough gold to go down in some dark tunnel in a place like this. But Jed convinced Grobennar to follow him down. And well, after some time, Grobennar came back up wearing that amulet and Jed came back . . . the way he is now."

He said this as if it explained everything.

Annoyed and eager to know more, Rajuban said, "And how is this Jed now?"

The boy's nervous expression returned. "Well . . . um . . . he's mute." Hector looked from side to side and whispered, "He don't speak no more."

Rajuban rolled his eyes. Yes, thank you for clarifying that.

"He's just not right in the head no more. Some bad spirit done broke his mind or somethin'. Grobennar says he thinks Jed just struck his head on a sharp rock, and there was a bloody wound when he come out, but we's all know the truth. Ain't no one goes near that place now."

Rajuban leaned in closer. "So no one went back to see what else was inside?"

"No sir. Nothin' worth that kind of trouble. Jed's parents tried to get the local Mazi to go investigate, but Mazi Ferodan said it wasn't worth the trip. Buncha' superstitious foolishness is what he said."

Rajuban thought for only a moment before he knew what needed to be done. It was a messy thing, but he saw no other way. He could leave no tracks here. Rajuban moved to sit beside the boy. "You're going to describe the location of this place in as much detail as possible right now. Can you do that for me, Hector?"

Kazi Ferodan spoke up, "Razir Rajuban, if it please you, I have matters elsewhere to attend to. May I have permission to take my leave?"

Rajuban scowled. "As a matter of fact, it would very much displease me to have you leave in the midst of such a revelation. No, you will stay."

Kazi Ferodan bowed, "My sincerest apologies, I intended no—"

"Save it," interrupted Rajuban. "Now, please, continue."

⊰⊰⊰

Rajuban kept the cowl of his hood pulled, hiding his face and the Klerósi robes beneath.

"The bodies are located in the western reaches of the muck quarter, not far from here." He described the specifics, then handed the man the golden coin. "You and your boys will deposit the bodies, weighed down by stones, in the river this very evening. Be discreet; that is what I'm paying you for, after all. You'll receive the other half tomorrow morning when the deed is done. And you will forget that this ever happened. Is this understood?"

The tall muscular man grunted. "Whatever you say. With this kind of gold, I'm happy to forget my own name."

"Good." Then Rajuban was gone. He had not enjoyed having to slay Kazi Ferodan, or the two boys, especially with his knives. Such dirty work. But doing the deed with Klerós's power would have drawn too much unwanted attention. If he was right about what he would find in that tunnel, his plans to rise to prominence were surely within his grasp. Grobennar could continue believing he was the only one with such an advantage, but Rajuban would win in the end.

Grobennar would never see it coming.

THANK YOU FOR READING

WORD-OF-MOUTH IS CRUCIAL FOR ANY author to succeed. If you enjoyed *To Earn the Sash*, please pay it forward by posting an honest review to Goodreads, Amazon, Bookbub, or wherever you post reviews.

Other works by Derrick Smythe include:

Passage to Dawn series
Book 1 | The Other Magic
Book 2 | The Other Way
Book 3 | The Other Battle (TBD)
Book 4 | The Other Truth (TBD)

Passage to Dawn companions
Prequel 1 | To Earn the Sash
Prequel 2 | To Wield a Plague

READ ON FOR A SNEAK PEEK OF

THE
OTHER
MAGIC

THE OTHER MAGIC

GROBENNAR

GROBENNAR'S EYES FLEW OPEN AS a loud boom rattled his bedchamber, rousing him from sleep. He immediately drew on the powers of his god, Klerós, prepared to vanquish the source of the disturbance. Then it came again: THUMP-THUMP-THUMP.

He sighed and relaxed, extinguishing his god's magic as he rose from the bed. Just a messenger. "Coming."

Grobennar instinctively snatched up the red-ruby pendant on his way to the door.

"Ooooh my. A missive so early in the morning? Whatever could this be?" came the familiar haunting voice in Grobennar's head, from the spirit trapped within the pendant, Jaween.

"I suspect we'll learn shortly." He shook out stiff limbs as he approached, rubbed his still sleepy face, then pulled open the door.

48

A palace soldier stood at attention, waiting respectfully for Grobennar to speak.

"Yes?"

The soldier gave a dutiful bow, face nearly touching the stone floor, and rightfully so in the presence of the High Priest. "The Lord King wishes to see you in his chambers at once, Your Grace."

Grobennar glanced out his bedroom window to confirm that it was indeed still dark outside. A summons before dawn?

Turning back to acknowledge the soldier, Grobennar grumbled, "Very well."

He strode across the room to his chest to retrieve a suitable robe, the one with the yellow embroidery, a subtle reminder of his position as Fatu Mazi, greatest among the priesthood. The God-king knew this, of course, but as his spiritual leader, Grobennar felt it necessary to always model perfected etiquette. The Lord ruler's endowed magical abilities were frighteningly powerful, but he lacked any feel for the formalities that came with leading the Empire. He had grown increasingly defiant in recent months, and Grobennar had resorted to simpler, indirect teachings through example.

"With the God-king's indignant mood as of late, perhaps it would be wise to stop at the kitchen for a pastry? Humans like pastries."

"Quiet," hissed Grobennar.

"Fine. Fine. I'm only trying to help. You know how much I like to be helpful."

Grobennar scurried down the narrow corridor toward the God-king's chambers, still dark but for the mystic flicker of red flames on either end. Grobennar's joints had shrugged off the stiffness that came with his thirty-seven years by the time he reached the guards outside the chambers.

The two men bowed deeply, then opened the massive oak doors to Magog's bedchamber, their expressions intense as they regained their positions at attention, prepared to dispatch unwelcome guests.

Grobennar entered and saw Magog seated at the edge of the bed, his bronze skin shaped by an imposing muscular body, shimmering with sweat, nude from the waist up. The God-king's long translucent hair hung wildly about his head, taking on the color of the flames around the room.

Grobennar bowed with minimal reverence, then continued his approach to stand before his Lord. "You requested my presence, Lord Magog?"

Magog's topaz eyes became narrow slits. They were surrounded by an increasing number of red scale-like growths mostly around his left eye, though a few had started around the right. These scales, reminders of his unusual birth and his growing power, were disconcerting and comforting at once.

He said, "I observed the crescent and the full moons crossing Lesante's gift this night."

Grobennar understood the implications of such signs. The founder of their faith, the last prophet, and her seers had foretold the Renewal, a purge of the unsaved world through force. This sign was said to mark the beginning. The crescent moon crossing its smaller counterpart at the center of the most well-known constellation was representative of the Lugienese Empire stretching their dominion to the ends of the world.

"You are certain of this?" asked Grobennar, skeptical as always. This astrological occurrence had been observed before, but the scholars had dismissed it, believing the location in the stars not centered enough within Lesante's gift to pass scrutiny.

Magog let out a breath of frustration. "Of course I am certain. The enemy has stirred. Last night I felt a presence, a wrongness. It was faint, but combined with these signs, the truth cannot be ignored."

Grobennar did not like the sound of this, for he had sensed nothing. "How can you be certain of what you felt? Perhaps your stomach simply did not agree with your evening meal."

Magog's frustration leaked through his voice. "I am certain! The Dark Lord's agent stirs; it is time to act!" He glared at Grobennar, daring him to disagree.

Grobennar knew better, yet the idea of rash action did not sit well with him. He was a believer. After having seen Magog's birth with his own eyes, how could he not be? And yet, these prophecies had been twisted over the years to fit situations that later proved imprudent. Grobennar remained straight-backed, knowing the importance of posture in projecting the credibility of his advice, something Magog had been less inclined to accept as of late.

"You are right to be prepared with the knowledge of the prophecies. You are, after all, the prophesied redeemer. Yet do these very same prophecies not speak of caution? Do they not speak of the importance of our preparations? I do not doubt your sincerity, of course, but perha—"

The words died in his throat as he felt the tingling sensation of magic, Magog's magic.

He wouldn't dare, I'm his—

A wave of power struck Grobennar like a line of fists and he careened into the stone wall across the room. The impact knocked his wind out.

Magog's booming voice followed—"I am done waiting! I am the God-king!"—penetrating deep into Grobennar's throbbing head.

Grobennar coughed and sucked in a deep breath of air. He crawled to his knees, angry at being attacked by the boy he had raised and trained from infancy. He began to rise to his feet.

"How dare you! I am your—"

Another blast of energy split the air. Grobennar used his own powers to deflect the blow, but the sheer volume of energy was too great and he was still thrown back into the wall. He landed with a thud, then groaned.

"You are my servant!" Magog's voice became a growl. "I am not yours to command. You have forgotten your place."

Never before had Magog lashed out like this. His powers were as of yet still manifesting, still growing, but already he commanded strength unknown to any mortal man. Magog could easily kill him if he wished, and Grobennar now feared that in his anger, he just might. He forgot the physical pain of the attack on his body, and the great blow to his ego.

"I—I am sorry, My Lord."

The voice in Grobennar's mind interrupted his already strained thoughts. "You're not alone with the God-king. I sense the life-essence of another; a wielder."

Grobennar collected himself and rose, forgetting the danger posed by the unpredictably obstinate God-king. It was still Grobennar's duty to serve and protect. Perhaps the God-king was right about the coming of the Dark Lord's agent. Grobennar drew in Klerós's power. Then he spotted movement to his right. He summoned more, ready to strike—

"What are—how dare you!" Magog yelled.

Grobennar ignored the oblivious Emperor as a form materialized from the shadows cast by ceiling-high drapes in the corner of the room. Grobennar shouted, "Get down!"

Grobennar extended a hand, readying to strike. Just before he released a bolt of searing energy, the shadowy shape stepped into the light and spoke. Grobennar recognized the voice with revulsion, relaxing his magic with reluctance.

Mazi Rajuban. A member of the High Council and long-standing opponent of both Grobennar and his more conservative faction within the Council. "Peace, brother. I was asked by the God-king to be in attendance for today's meeting."

Jaween spoke into Grobennar's mind, "Have I mentioned that I do not care for this man?"

Nor do I, thought Grobennar wryly to himself.

His own anger reignited. That's what Rajuban wishes. Grobennar forced himself to relent. "Of course. The God-king is wise to seek the wisdom of a member of the High Council. Yet perhaps this is a matter for the collective wisdom of the High Council to discuss in its entirety."

The God-king bellowed, "The High Council is fickle, paralytic, and incapable of action!" Lowering his voice, he added, "You are right about assembling the Council. But it will not be to initiate discourse. You will inform them." He raised his voice once more. "You will inform them that the time has at long last come to begin preparations for the Purge. The enemy stirs! We too must shed our idle position."

Grobennar knew better than to disagree. He had somehow lost favor with the God-king, and Rajuban's attendance here served as an answer to the question of how.

"Yes, Lord. It shall be done."

Rajuban smiled. "You are wise to see the wisdom of the God-king's words. He has been tightly leashed for far too long. The time has come for him to realize his true destiny as avatar to Klerós, praise be his name."

"Oh he's good. I can't help but hate him, but his politics are praiseworthy. Perhaps we might torture and kill him later?"

Grobennar ignored Jaween, instead looking to Magog, nodding. The decision had been made. Rajuban had defeated him in this bout.

"Of course. This is well. Klerós guide the both of you."

That snake had maneuvered behind his back to gain the ear of the God-king. He would need to tread very carefully.

Grobennar bade the God-king farewell, refusing to acknowledge Rajuban, then stalked out of the room as quickly as possible. He considered his next course of action, though there wasn't much to consider. He had no choice but to call a full assembly as instructed.

Grobennar entered his own chambers and melted into the chair beside his bed, mentally exhausted.

"So. This purge. That means war, right? I will be able to persuade our enemies?"

Grobennar picked up a quill and ink from the small table to his left to begin writing out a list of preparations. "Yes, the Purge means war. I suspect you'll have plenty of chances to persuade, you might even see some killing."

"Ooh-ooh-ooh. Yes, persuading and killing! I know your mood is a touch soured from earlier, but this really does call for celebration. A small feast, perhaps? That might lighten your mood, as well."

Grobennar ignored Jaween.

"Did you write that down?"

Grobennar continued to work on his list.

"Are you ignoring me again? You know it hurts my feelings when you ignore me."

Grobennar reached up and removed the pendant from his neck and tossed it onto his bed a few paces away, limiting the strength of the spirit's connection to him. "I need to think," he said through clenched teeth.

He wondered if perhaps secreting the forbidden spirit from the debris all those years ago had resulted in more trouble than it was worth. He heard a sound in his head that was disturbingly not like weeping, yet he knew from his time with Jaween that this was precisely what the spirit was intending to communicate.

He sighed. "I'm not ignoring you, Jaween. You can stop the crying. I just need it quiet in order to think."

Jaween's mood elevated. "So that sounded like real crying this time, didn't it?"

Grobennar rolled his eyes. "Closer than ever before."

It was going to be a very long day.

About the Author

DERRICK SMYTHE HAS BEEN FASCINATED with all things elvish, dwarvish, and magical since his days of running through the woods with sharpened sticks in defense of whatever fortification he and his brothers had built that summer. After consuming nearly every fantasy book he could find, he was driven to begin work on one of his own. When he isn't dreaming up new stories, he can be spotted hiking the Adirondack Mountains or traveling the world. He currently resides near his hometown in upstate New York with his enchanting wife, ethereal daughters, and his faithful-if-neurotic Australian Shepherd, Magnus.

Derricks Smythe's debut novel, *The Other Magic*, is the award-winning first installment of his passage to dawn series, an epic fantasy set in the World of Doréa.

To learn more about Derrick and his work visit:
Website: derricksmythe.com
Facebook: derricksmythe.author
Email: author@derricksmythe.com